Chill on the Hill

"Let's have a hot chocolate," Bess suggested.

"Good idea," Molly agreed.

Nancy, Bess, George, and Molly climbed up the hill and left their sleds under a big tree. Bess led the way to the hot-chocolate van.

When the girls finished their hot chocolate, they walked back to where they'd left their sleds.

"Oh, no," Molly said right away. "My sled is gone!"

She was right. Nancy saw four sleds under the tree. One was hers, one was George's, and one was Bess's. But the fourth sled definitely *wasn't* Molly's.

The Nancy Drew Notebooks

\# 1 The Slumber Party Secret
\# 2 The Lost Locket
\# 3 The Secret Santa
\# 4 Bad Day for Ballet
\# 5 The Soccer Shoe Clue
\# 6 The Ice Cream Scoop
\# 7 Trouble at Camp Treehouse
\# 8 The Best Detective
\# 9 The Thanksgiving Surprise
\#10 Not Nice on Ice
\#11 The Pen Pal Puzzle
\#12 The Puppy Problem
\#13 The Wedding Gift Goof
\#14 The Funny Face Fight
\#15 The Crazy Key Clue
\#16 The Ski Slope Mystery
\#17 Whose Pet Is Best?
\#18 The Stolen Unicorn
\#19 The Lemonade Raid
\#20 Hannah's Secret
\#21 Princess on Parade
\#22 The Clue in the Glue
\#23 Alien in the Classroom
\#24 The Hidden Treasures
\#25 Dare at the Fair
\#26 The Lucky Horseshoes
\#27 Trouble Takes the Cake
\#28 Thrill on the Hill

Available from MINSTREL Books

THE
NANCY DREW
NOTEBOOKS®

#28

Thrill on the Hill

CAROLYN KEENE
ILLUSTRATED BY ANTHONY ACCARDO

A MINSTREL® BOOK

Published by POCKET BOOKS
New York   London   Toronto   Sydney   Tokyo   Singapore

This book is a work of fiction. Names, characters, places and incidents are products of the author's imagination or are used fictitiously. Any resemblance to actual events or locales or persons living or dead is entirely coincidental.

A MINSTREL PAPERBACK *Original*

 A Minstrel Book published by
POCKET BOOKS, a division of Simon & Schuster Inc.
1230 Avenue of the Americas, New York, NY 10020

ISBN: 0-671-02492-2

First Minstrel Books printing January 1999

10   9   8   7   6   5   4   3   2   1

NANCY DREW, THE NANCY DREW NOTEBOOKS,
A MINSTREL BOOK and colophon are registered trademarks of
Simon & Schuster Inc.

Cover art by Joanie Schwarz

Printed in the U.S.A.

QBP/

Thrill on the Hill

1

Ten Inches of Snow

Wow!" eight-year-old Nancy Drew exclaimed. She was looking out her bedroom window. A thick layer of snow covered the grass, the trees, and the houses. The rose bushes in the yard were completely buried. The snow had fallen during the night, while Nancy was sleeping.

Nancy dressed for school as quickly as possible. She ran downstairs.

Her father was sitting at the kitchen table. Hannah Gruen, the Drews' housekeeper, was working at the counter. She had taken care of Nancy ever since her mother died, five years earlier.

"Good morning, Daddy," Nancy said. "Hi, Hannah. Isn't the snow great?"

"Good morning, Pudding Pie," Mr. Drew replied. "We got ten inches last night."

"Cool," Nancy said. She slipped into her chair at the table.

"Your school may be closed," Hannah told Nancy. She turned up the radio. "Let's listen to the news report."

Nancy began eating her toast and scrambled eggs. She listened as the radio announcer read a long list of schools that were closed because of the snow.

"Carl Sandburg Elementary School," the announcer said.

"Yippee!" Nancy yelled. "No school! May I please go sledding in the park?"

"Why not?" Mr. Drew said with a smile. "I'll get your sled out of the basement."

"Great," Nancy said.

After breakfast she called her friends George Fayne and Bess Marvin. They agreed to meet at Nancy's house as soon as possible.

Half an hour later, the girls were pulling their sleds through the deep snow. Each step took a lot of energy. It took the girls almost ten minutes to get to the end of Nancy's street.

"Pulling a sled in the snow is hard," Bess said. She had the same kind of sled as Nancy—a wooden one with runners.

"I think it's fun," George said. She had a blue saucer sled.

Nancy smiled. Sometimes it was difficult to believe her best friends were cousins. They were so different.

Bess's blond hair was neatly pulled back with a hair band. She was careful not to fall down. Bess didn't like her clothes to get dirty. George was taller with dark, curly hair. She liked sports more than Bess did. Even though the girls were different, they had tons of fun together.

Nancy was happy when the girls

finally reached the park. Near the entrance, a woman was selling hot chocolate from a van.

"Hilda's Hot Chocolate," Nancy read off the van's side. "We'll have to come back here later. Daddy gave me some money."

"We can drink hot chocolate to warm up," George said. "But we have to get cold first!"

The girls walked into the park. They stood at the top of a long hill and looked down. Dozens of kids were sledding. Nancy spotted some boys from her class: Mike Minelli, Jason Hutchings, and David Berger.

"Here comes Molly," Bess said.

Molly Angelo was marching up the hill. She was dragging her sled behind her. Molly was in the same class as Nancy, Bess, and George. She was a small, bouncy girl with long, curly dark hair.

"Wait for me!" Molly called to the others. "We can go down the hill together!"

"Okay," Nancy called. She positioned her sled on the top of the hill and sat down on it. She kept her feet on the ground so she wouldn't start sliding.

"I'm ready!" Molly announced. Her sled had hand brakes, a plastic seat, and wide runners.

"Me, too!" George said.

"Just a second," Bess said. She was still fussing with her gloves and scarf.

Nancy gave Bess another minute to get ready. Then she pushed off.

"Catch me if you can!" Nancy yelled. She laughed as she bumped over the snow. Her sled went faster and faster. The wind was blowing in her eyes.

Near the bottom, Molly zoomed past Nancy. Her sled went farther than Nancy's, too.

George and Bess stopped behind Nancy.

"That was fun!" George said as she climbed off her sled.

"Yeah!" Molly said.

"I got snow on my clothes," Bess said. But she was smiling.

"Let's go again," Nancy said. She led the way up the hill.

"Your sled is fast," George told Molly.

"I know," Molly said. "I just got it for my birthday. You guys can try it, if you like."

"Okay," Nancy agreed.

On the next run, Nancy and Molly switched sleds. Then George took a turn on Molly's sled. They were coming up the hill for the fourth time when Rebecca Ramirez called their names.

Rebecca lived near Nancy. They walked to school together. Rebecca wanted to be an actress when she grew up. She made a big drama out of everything.

"Hi, Rebecca!" Nancy called. "Where's your sled?"

"My dumb brother has it," Rebecca said with a heavy sigh. Rebecca's brother, Todd, was twelve years old.

"How come?" George asked.

"It's *so* unfair," Rebecca said. "Todd didn't take good care of his sled last winter. The runners rusted. Now Mom is making me share with him. Only, Todd disappeared. I haven't seen him or my sled for half an hour."

"Maybe he went to the Gulch," Nancy said. The Gulch was a steeper hill about half a mile away. Older kids liked to sled there.

"Probably," Rebecca said. "I bet I'll never see my sled again!"

"You can have a turn on mine," Bess offered.

"Thanks," Rebecca said.

For the next hour, the five girls shared four sleds. Nancy thought Molly's was the most fun because it went fastest.

Nancy was waiting for her friends at the top of the hill when some older kids arrived. She recognized Sam McCorry.

Sam was wearing a jacket that said River Heights High School Football.

Nancy knew Sam because she played with his younger sister sometimes.

"This hill is tiny," Sam told his friends.

"Let's do a few runs and then go to the Gulch," one of Sam's friends said.

"Sounds good," Sam said. "Beat you to the bottom!" He pushed off hard and started down the hill. His sled was exactly the same as Molly's.

Sam's going too fast, Nancy thought. And he's headed directly for Bess!

Bess was just climbing off her sled at the bottom of the hill.

"Watch out, Bess!" Nancy shouted.

2

No Marshmallows

ancy's warning came too late.

Sam plowed right into Bess. Bess fell backward into the snow.

"Bess!" Nancy shouted. She ran down the hill. George, Rebecca, and Molly came running, too. Bess was lying on her side. She looked hurt.

Nancy bent down next to Bess. "Are you okay?" she asked.

"I—I guess so," Bess said. She slowly sat up and rubbed her leg.

Sam walked over. "Is anything broken?" he asked.

"No," Bess said angrily. "But my leg hurts. You should be more careful."

"I'm sorry," Sam said. He held out his hand. "Here. Let me help you up."

Bess let Sam pull her to her feet. She brushed the snow off her clothes.

Sam's friends came up with their sleds.

"Nice control!" a boy in a brown ski cap teased Sam.

"That race doesn't count," a girl with red hair told him.

Sam seemed to forget all about Bess. "Why not?" he asked. "I beat you by a mile."

"You also knocked down a little kid," the girl said. "So it doesn't count."

"Fine," Sam said. "We'll race again. And I'll beat you again."

"You're on," the girl said.

Sam and his friends rushed off for the top of the hill.

"They weren't very worried about me," Bess said in a grumpy voice. "And they called me a little kid!"

George gave Bess a pat on the shoulder. "Come on," she said. "You're not hurt. Forget about Sam. Let's go for another run."

"No thanks," Bess said. "I'm staying as far away from Sam McCorry as possible. As long as he's sledding here, I'm not."

"I have to head home anyway," Rebecca said. "My mom—" She stopped talking because her brother had sledded up to them.

"Hey, Rebecca," Todd said. "You can have your sled now. I'm going to build a snowman with my friends."

"I don't want it," Rebecca said. "I'm going home now."

"Too bad," Todd said. "It's your turn."

Todd headed up the hill. He left the sled at Rebecca's feet.

"This is *so* unfair," Rebecca said. "I pulled the sled here. Todd rode it all morning. And now I have to take it home!"

"Why don't you stay awhile?" Nancy asked.

"I can't," Rebecca said. "Mom wants me to help her shovel the walks."

"Too bad," Nancy said.

"Let's have a hot chocolate now," Bess suggested. "Maybe Sam will be gone by the time we finish."

"Good idea," Molly agreed.

The girls climbed up the hill. Rebecca headed for home. The other girls left their sleds under a big tree. Bess led the way to the hot-chocolate van.

The woman inside peered out at them. She had gray hair pulled back in a sloppy bun. Her eyebrows were bushy. Her eyes were small and dark.

"Are you Hilda?" Nancy asked.

"What?" the woman shouted. She cupped a hand behind her ear and leaned closer.

"Are you Hilda?" Nancy said louder.

"That's me," Hilda said in a grouchy voice. "How many?"

"Four," Nancy said.

"That will be two dollars," Hilda said.

Nancy paid. Hilda took her money without saying "thank you." While she fixed the cups of hot chocolate, she talked into a phone that was tucked between her ear and shoulder.

"The van needs new tires," Hilda yelled. She passed the cups out to the girls. "*Four* new tires! And I don't have enough money for even one!"

"Come on," Molly said, pointing to a park bench. "Let's go sit over there. I don't want to hear Hilda screaming."

The others nodded. They walked over to the bench, brushed off the snow, and sat down.

Nancy took a sip of her hot chocolate. "Yuck," she said. "This hot chocolate tastes like water."

George made a face. "Maybe some marshmallows would help," she suggested. "I'll go ask Hilda if she has any."

The other girls waited while George went back to the van. She returned quickly.

15

"Sorry," George said. "I couldn't get any marshmallows. Hilda isn't in the van."

"That's okay," Molly said.

"It doesn't taste *too* bad if you hold your nose," Bess said.

The girls finished most of their hot chocolate. They put their cups in a trash bin. Then they walked back to where they'd left their sleds.

"Oh, no," Molly said right away. "My sled is gone!"

She was right. Nancy saw four sleds under the tree. One was hers, one was George's, and one was Bess's. But the fourth sled definitely *wasn't* Molly's. It was a beat-up saucer. Even the pink rope attached to it looked old.

"My earmuffs are gone, too," Molly said. She sounded as if she was about to cry. "I left them tucked under my sled."

"It looks like you've been robbed," George said.

"Well, I want my sled back," Molly said. "I'll offer a reward to whoever finds it. I'll, um, give them my secret snow ice cream recipe."

Nancy felt bad for Molly. But she was also excited. She loved to solve mysteries, and she was good at it.

"I don't understand," Bess said. "Who would want Molly's sled? All of the kids here already have their own."

"Not Todd," Nancy said.

"That's right," George said. "He could have taken Molly's sled because he hates sharing with Rebecca."

"Look!" Nancy said. "Those sled tracks are extra fat. They look like they might have been made with the runners on your sled, Molly."

Molly bent down for a closer look. "I'm pretty sure those tracks *were* made by my sled," she said.

"Let's see where they lead," Nancy said. The girls followed the tracks through the snow to the sidewalk. But then the tracks blended in with lots of footprints.

Nancy turned in a circle. "Whoever dragged Molly's sled up here could have been getting into a car."

"Or a van!" Molly exclaimed. "The hot-chocolate van is only a few yards away."

"Hilda could have taken the sled," George said. "She could sell it for the money she needs to buy new tires."

Nancy was thinking about that when something hit her in the back of the head!

3

Another Suspect

"Someone hit me with a snowball," Nancy said. She rubbed the back of her head.

"Who?" George asked. At that second, another snowball hit her right in the face!

"It was Mike Minelli!" Bess yelled, pointing. "I saw him. He's right behind that tree."

"Jason Hutchings is with him!" Molly added. "David Berger, too!"

"We'd better get under cover," Nancy called. The girls ran to a park bench, and hid behind it.

"Don't let the boys hit me," Bess said. "I don't want to get snow in my hair."

"You and Molly make snowballs," George said. "Nancy and I will throw them."

The boys pitched snowballs at them from behind the trees. Nancy and George threw back.

Nancy hit Mike right in the chest. "Bull's-eye!" she yelled.

"Attack!" David yelled. The boys ran toward the girls' bench, throwing snowballs as quickly as possible.

But Bess and Molly had lots of snowballs piled up. All four girls threw as fast as they could. They hit the boys with one snowball after another.

"Run away!" Jason yelled to the other boys.

"We'll get you next time!" Mike called.

"Four against three isn't fair anyway!" David hollered.

George laughed as she flopped down on the bench. "We showed them!"

"That was fun," Nancy said.

"Yeah," Bess said. "Except that my gloves are soaked!"

Molly rolled her eyes. "I didn't think it was so much fun. Mike Minelli is always playing jokes on me. I'm sick of it."

Mike *was* always clowning around, Nancy thought. He'd put spaghetti down her shirt once. And he had tried to scare Nancy and her friends when they were having a slumber party at Rebecca's house.

"Do you guys think Mike might have taken Molly's sled?" Nancy asked. "It could be another one of his practical jokes."

"But Mike was just here," Bess said. "If he'd stolen the sled, we would have seen it."

"Maybe yes, maybe no," Molly said. "Mike could have put the sled up in a tree. He might have taken it back to my garage. Or he could have buried it under three feet of snow. That's the kind of thing Mike thinks is funny."

Nancy nodded. "Let's add Mike to our list of suspects," she said. "We can watch him tomorrow at school."

"*If* we don't find Molly's sled before then," George said.

"And if we even *have* school tomorrow," Bess added. "Maybe it will be another snow day."

"Maybe," Nancy agreed. "But even if we don't see Mike at school, we know where he lives. But we *don't* know how to find Hilda."

"Nancy's right," Molly said. "Hilda could just drive away and take my sled with her."

"We'd better search around the van for clues right now," Nancy said. "Before it's too late."

The girls began to walk toward the van. "I hope Hilda doesn't see us," Bess said. "She was grouchy before. I bet she'll be really mad if she catches us snooping."

"That's true," Nancy said. "Maybe you and George should distract Hilda while Molly and I look for clues."

The others agreed. When they got to the van, George and Bess went to the little window where they had ordered. There were no other people buying hot chocolate.

Molly and Nancy tiptoed around the back of the van.

"Look," Molly whispered. "The doors are open."

"What super luck," Nancy said. "Now we can see inside."

Nancy peeked into the van. The seats were gone. The space inside was set up as a tiny kitchen. Nancy saw a row of cabinets above a small counter. Under the counter was a little refrigerator. A microwave oven sat on the countertop. There was even a miniature sink. Way in the front of the van, Nancy could see two seats and the steering wheel.

"Where's Hilda?" Nancy whispered. She wasn't in the little kitchen or in the front of the van.

Just then George and Bess joined Nancy and Molly. "Hilda isn't here," George reported.

"What should we do now?" Bess asked.

"Keep watch," Nancy said. "Let us know if she comes back."

"Okay!" George and Bess walked back around the side of the van.

"Do you see my sled?" Molly whispered.

"No," Nancy said. "But there are lots of hiding places inside the van. Maybe we should climb in to get a better look."

"What if Hilda comes back?" Molly asked.

Nancy thought for a moment. "Then we'll just have to tell her the truth," she said. "But let's hope she doesn't come back."

Molly swallowed hard. "Well . . . okay. If you think this is the only way we can find my sled."

"I do," Nancy said. She pulled herself into the back of the van. Molly followed her.

Nancy peeked into the first cabinet. It was much too small to hide a sled.

"Hurry up," Molly whispered.

Nancy crept forward a little more. She looked behind the seats. No sled back here, Nancy thought.

Just then she heard a sound: footsteps. Heavy footsteps that sounded as if they could be Hilda's! Nancy's heart started beating double time.

"What's that?" Molly asked. Her eyes were wide with fear.

"It sounds like Hilda," Nancy said. "But it can't be her. George and Bess would have warned us."

But just then the van's back door slammed.

"What do we do now?" Molly whispered.

4

A Close Call

We have to get out of here," Nancy told Molly quietly. Her heart was pounding.

"How?" Molly asked.

Nancy was certain Hilda would get into the van soon. She would easily discover the girls. Nancy wasn't sure what Hilda would do to them. And she didn't want to find out.

I have to find a way for us to escape without Hilda seeing us, Nancy thought.

"Try the rear doors," Nancy whispered to Molly. "But don't make too much noise."

Molly tiptoed back to the doors. She gently tried to turn the handle. It didn't budge.

Nancy peeked out the serving window.

She was careful because she wasn't sure where Hilda had gone.

Bess and George were standing just outside the window. When Bess spotted Nancy, she started jumping up and down. Without making a sound, George pointed to the front of the van.

"Come on!" Nancy whispered. She grabbed Molly's hand and pulled her toward the front passenger door.

Nancy crawled onto the seat, opened the door, and hopped out. Molly was right behind her.

George gently closed the door. It made a tiny clicking sound as the lock caught.

"Where's Hilda?" Nancy whispered.

"On the other side of the van," George told her.

A minute later Hilda opened the driver's door. The girls could hear her muttering to herself. They tiptoed farther away.

Nancy and her friends reached the

sidewalk. The van's motor started up. Hilda drove off without even looking at the girls.

"Whew!" Nancy said. "That was close."

"Do you think she knew we were inside?" Molly asked.

"No," Nancy said.

"Was the sled in there?" Bess asked.

"Definitely not," Nancy told her. "We can cross Hilda off our suspects list." She giggled. "At least, I'll do that as soon as I *write* the suspects list."

Nancy's father had given her a special notebook with a shiny blue cover. She kept notes on all of her mysteries inside. But Nancy hadn't brought her notebook sledding. She planned to write down her suspects and clues as soon as she got home.

"I think it's time to go," Bess said. "I can hear my stomach growling!"

Molly looked sad. "I never thought I'd be going home without my new sled.

My parents are going to be mad when they find out it was stolen."

"Don't worry," Nancy said. "I'm sure we can find it."

Walking home was easier than walking to the park. Lots of people had shoveled their sidewalks. Plows were clearing the roads. More cars were moving.

When Nancy got home, Hannah fixed lunch. Nancy ate two bowls of tomato soup. Then she ate a turkey sandwich. Sledding all morning had made her extra hungry.

After lunch Nancy helped Hannah clean up the kitchen. Then she got out her blue notebook. She brought it to the table.

Nancy turned to a clean page. She wrote: "The Case of the Missing Sled." Under that she wrote: "Clues: Sled tracks leading toward the street."

Hannah was sorting through a big stack of mail. "Do you have a new mystery?" she asked.

"Yes," Nancy said. "Molly's sled is

31

missing. I have to find it before the snow melts."

"Why is that?" Hannah asked.

"Two reasons," Nancy said. "One is that Molly can't have any fun in the snow without her sled. And the other is that Molly is going to give her special snow ice cream recipe to whoever finds it."

Hannah smiled. "Well, I bet that will be you."

Nancy turned to a new page in her notebook. She wrote: "Suspects." She skipped a line and added: "Todd Ramirez. Needs a new sled. Mike Minelli. Likes to play jokes on Molly. Hilda, the hot-chocolate woman. Needs money for new tires." Then Nancy crossed Hilda's name off the list.

Too bad Dad isn't home, Nancy thought. Carson Drew often gave Nancy suggestions for solving mysteries. And right now she was wondering what to do next.

Nancy started to ask herself questions. Was there any way she could find out if Todd or Mike had Molly's sled? If they had taken it, where was it now?

That question gave Nancy an idea. "May I go over to Rebecca's?" she asked Hannah. "I think she can help me with the mystery."

"Sure," Hannah said. "But don't be gone long. It will be dark in a few hours."

"Okay," Nancy agreed. She pulled on her boots, jacket, hat, scarf, and mittens. Then she walked the few blocks to Rebecca's.

Rebecca answered the door. "Nancy!" she exclaimed. "It's *so* great to see you. Come in!"

Nancy giggled. Rebecca was being dramatic again. "I just saw you this morning," she reminded her friend.

"That's true," Rebecca admitted. She led Nancy upstairs to her room. "But I've been bored all afternoon. I hope we have school tomorrow. Staying home all day is a drag!"

Nancy started taking off her outdoor clothes. "Well, something exciting happened after you left the park," she said. She told Rebecca about Molly's missing sled.

"Poor Molly," Rebecca said. "That sled was really cool. Much nicer than mine. Who do you think took it?"

"Well . . . promise not to get mad," Nancy said.

"I promise," Rebecca said.

"I was wondering if Todd might have taken it," Nancy said. "His sled is ruined."

"And he totally hates sharing a sled with me," Rebecca said. "Except I hate sharing with him even more."

"Do you think he—" Nancy started.

Rebecca gasped. "Wait! When did the sled disappear?"

Nancy thought about it. "A few hours ago. Not long after you left the park."

Rebecca nodded. "That's what I thought. Guess what I saw this afternoon?"

"What?" Nancy asked.

"Todd!" Rebecca exclaimed. "I saw him through the kitchen window. He was in the garage."

"So what?" Nancy asked.

"So, I bet he was hiding the sled in there!" Rebecca said.

5

In the Garage

Let's go out to the garage," Nancy said. "If Todd hid Molly's sled out there, it shouldn't be too hard to find."

Rebecca looked a little pale. "There's just one problem with that plan," she said.

"What?" Nancy asked.

"I never, ever go into the garage," Rebecca whispered.

"Why not?" Nancy asked.

"It's haunted!" Rebecca said. Her eyes were wide.

"Haunted?" Nancy repeated. "What makes you think that?"

"Spooky noises," Rebecca said. "I heard them last time I took out the trash. I yelled so loudly that the neighbors came running. After that, Mom made taking out the trash Todd's job."

Nancy giggled. "Aren't you worried the ghost will get *him?*" she asked.

Rebecca shook her head. "Better him than me," she said.

Nancy thought for a moment. "Todd knows you're scared of the garage," she said. "That makes it the perfect place for him to hide Molly's sled. We *have* to go out there to look around."

"What about the ghost?" Rebecca asked.

"I don't believe in ghosts," Nancy said.

"Well, I do!" Rebecca said.

"Don't worry," Nancy told her. "You don't have to come with me."

Rebecca sighed heavily. "That's okay," she said. "I'll come. It's too dangerous for you to go alone. And I'd feel awful if something happened to you."

"Okay," Nancy said. She wasn't scared. Well, maybe she was a *little*. Anyway, she thought it would be nice to have Rebecca with her.

Nancy and Rebecca bundled up in their coats, boots, hats, and gloves. Then Rebecca led the way out to her garage. She walked very slowly—as if she wasn't in any hurry to get there.

The garage was a small building separate from the Ramirez family's house. It was painted mud brown.

Rebecca lifted a latch on one of the garage's big double doors. *Crrreak*, the hinge moaned as the door swung open.

Nancy shuddered. Goose bumps rose on her arms. "This garage *is* creepy," she told Rebecca.

Rebecca nodded. "Come on," she whispered. "Let's look fast and get out of here."

"Okay," Nancy agreed. She took a few steps into the garage. Rebecca's family had piled up lots of old tools, toys, and cardboard boxes. The air smelled dusty. Dried leaves were scattered on the floor. Ragged spiderwebs covered the windows.

This isn't the kind of garage you go into without a reason, Nancy thought. That made her even more curious about why Todd had come out there.

"It's already starting to get dark outside," Nancy said. "Is there a light?"

"Kind of," Rebecca said. She flicked a switch. A lightbulb up near the garage's roof went on. But the light was very dim.

"That's not much help," Nancy said. She felt uneasy as she looked into the dark building. Going into a haunted garage was bad. Going into a *dark* haunted garage was *awful*.

"Mom keeps a flashlight around here somewhere," Rebecca said. She reached down by the floor. "Here it is!"

"Great!" Nancy said, trying to sound unafraid. "Lead the way."

"Me?" Rebecca said. "No way! You lead."

"Well, okay," Nancy said. She took the flashlight from Rebecca and tiptoed into the garage.

Rebecca crept along right behind her.

Nancy shone the flashlight on a lawn mower, a can of brown paint, a stack of old paperback books . . .

Scrrrff . . . Scrrrff.

Rebecca grabbed Nancy's arm. "Did you hear that?" she whispered. Her voice sounded shaky. "That's the sound the ghost makes! I knew we shouldn't come out here."

Nancy's heart was beating fast. I don't believe in ghosts, she told herself. I don't believe in ghosts.

Nancy swallowed hard. Her mouth felt dry. "I think the sound came from behind the lawn mower," she said. "Maybe it was some leaves blowing across the floor."

"Maybe," Rebecca said. She still sounded scared. "Or maybe it was a visitor from beyond the grave!"

Nancy shook her head. "Don't be silly," she said. "Come on. We're almost finished." She crept inside a few more steps. She shone the flashlight on some gardening tools, an old high chair, and a mostly flat soccer ball.

"Hey—look at that!" Rebecca cried. She pointed to the ground. Nancy saw some pieces of wood and metal. They were spread out on an old towel.

"That must be Molly's sled!" Rebecca exclaimed. "Todd broke it into a gazillion pieces!"

At first Nancy thought Rebecca was right. But then she noticed something.

"Wait a second," Nancy said. She shone the light on the pieces and got closer. The pieces were definitely part of a sled. But the metal parts were covered with red rust. And the bright paint had worn off the wooden pieces.

"I don't think this is Molly's sled," Nancy said.

"Why not?" Rebecca asked.

"Molly's sled was brand new," Nancy said. "But these parts are old and rusty. I bet Todd came out here this afternoon to clean up his old sled."

"That's possible," Rebecca said. "Mom told him she was never, ever buying him another one. And I'm not sharing with him after today."

Nancy was just straightening up when she heard that sound again.

Scrrrff. Scrrrff.

Nancy's heart started going bump, bump. Bump, bump. Somehow she knew she wasn't hearing blowing leaves. She started to back up.

"I just saw something!" Rebecca said. She grabbed the flashlight. She shone it back behind the lawn mower.

Nancy gasped. Something was reflecting the light back at them—a pair of red eyes!

6

Garage Ghost

Rebecca screamed. She dropped the flashlight. "It's the ghost!" she yelled. "Run for your life!"

"Wait!" Nancy called. But Rebecca had already raced outside.

Now Nancy was all alone in the dark garage. All alone, except for whoever— or whatever—those red eyes belonged to. Nancy wanted to run, too. But she didn't.

Instead, she took a deep breath, stepped forward, and picked up the flashlight. Its beam was fainter now. Nancy crept closer to the lawn mower and shone the light around.

There! The light picked out something. It was a brown-and-white animal with delicate paws. Nancy let out her breath in a rush.

"Rebecca!" she called. "It's only a raccoon!"

The raccoon scampered back behind the trash cans. *Scrrrff. Scrrrff.* That was the sound the raccoon's claws made against the concrete.

"I don't care!" Rebecca called. "It's getting dark, and I'm too scared to go back in there."

"Okay," Nancy called. "I'm coming out. It's not safe to get close to a raccoon." She gave the garage one more quick look. There was no sign of Molly's sled.

Nancy walked outside. "Well, I didn't find the sled," she told Rebecca. "But I did find your ghost. You should tell your parents about the raccoon. I bet he likes your trash."

"I'll tell them," Rebecca said. "But I still think the garage is haunted!"

*   *   *

Before going to bed that evening, Nancy got out her blue notebook. She looked at her suspects list again.

Hilda, the hot-chocolate woman, was crossed off. And now Nancy was pretty sure Todd hadn't taken the sled either. That left only Mike Minelli.

Nancy climbed into bed and turned out the bedside lamp. Mike Minelli was a big pain sometimes. But Nancy didn't think he would steal anything—unless he thought it was some sort of joke. Would Mike think stealing Molly's sled was funny?

There was only one way to find out. Nancy needed more clues. She hoped school would be open the next day. School was the perfect place for her to watch her prime suspect.

The next morning Nancy's backyard was still buried in snow. But the radio announcer said the roads were clear. School was open.

Nancy kept half an eye on Mike that morning. But she didn't have much time to think about the mystery.

Mrs. Reynolds, Nancy's teacher, wanted to make up for the snow day. The morning started with math problems. Next, the students did a science experiment about sound waves. Then Mrs. Reynolds asked them to write a paragraph. The topic was "I wish . . ."

"I wish it was time for lunch," Bess whispered to Nancy.

Nancy giggled. Then she got to work. "I wish I could find Molly's sled," she wrote. The rest of her paragraph was about how Molly's sled had disappeared.

Mrs. Reynolds collected the papers. The class went to lunch. When they got back, the paragraphs were hanging up in the hallway.

Nancy noticed one paper right away. Someone had drawn a sled! She got closer so that she could read the name.

"Look!" Nancy said to George, Bess,

and Molly. "Mike wishes he could have a new sled."

"That proves he took mine!" Molly said.

"No, it doesn't," Bess said. "It proves he *didn't* take yours. If Mike had your sled, he wouldn't need another one."

"Wait," Nancy said. "Let's read the rest of Mike's paragraph." George, Bess, and Molly read over Nancy's shoulder.

Mike's paragraph described a sled he'd seen in a toy store. It didn't sound anything like Molly's. The sled was bright yellow with racing stripes. The runners were made from a special metal, and it had a horn.

"Why would you need a horn on a sled?" George wondered.

"So that old ladies and little kids can get out of my way," Mike said. He ran by Molly. "Zrroom! Zrroom!"

"Cut it out," Molly told him.

"Cut it out," Mike repeated.

"Molly has a pretty cool sled," Nancy said to Mike.

Mike shrugged. "The same kind David has."

"Wouldn't you like a sled like that?" Nancy asked.

"David's sled is okay," Mike said. "But the one at the toy store was superhero cool! Besides, David's sled is too hard to steer."

Mike pretended he was steering a race car. He screeched to a stop next to his desk and sat down.

"Do you believe he doesn't like my sled?" Molly asked Nancy.

"Yes," Nancy said.

"So that proves Mike didn't take it," George said. "And that means we're out of suspects."

Molly shook her head. "I still think Mike took my sled," she said. "He just did it as a joke, not to keep."

"But your sled hasn't turned up covered with gumdrops or *Moleheads from Mars* stickers," Bess said. "If Mike was planning something sneaky, wouldn't he have done it by now?"

"Maybe yes, maybe no," Molly said. "But just in case it was someone else, I'm going to hang up lost-sled posters after school. I want everyone to know I'm offering a reward. Will you guys help me?"

"Sure," Nancy said.

Bess and George agreed, too.

After school the girls went over to Molly's house. Mrs. Angelo had made a big stack of lost-sled posters at work.

"We can hang more signs if we split up," Molly said.

"Good idea," George said. "Bess and I can cover Main Street."

Bess smiled. "Perfect," she said. "We can window-shop at the same time."

George groaned. "*You* do the window shopping," she said. "*I'll* take care of the posters."

Nancy and Molly began hanging posters near Molly's house. They taped them to streetlight poles. Nancy asked people they passed if they had seen Molly's sled. Nobody had.

Molly walked more and more slowly. "I bet we never find my sled," she said.

"I bet we do," Nancy said. "I think I just found a clue!"

7

A Sporty Snowman

Nancy pointed across the street. "Do you see what I see?" she asked.

Molly shrugged. "I see Melissa Adams. She's shoveling the walk in front of her house. But what does that have to do with my sled?"

"Check out the snowman in Melissa's yard," Nancy said.

The snowman stood under a big oak tree. He was a little taller than Nancy. He had gumdrop eyes, a carrot nose, a scarf around his neck—and he was wearing purple earmuffs.

"Hey!" Molly said. "Those look like *my* earmuffs."

"I think so, too," Nancy said.

"So you think Melissa took my sled?" Molly asked.

"No," Nancy said. "I just—"

Molly wasn't listening. "Come on!" she said angrily. "I want to talk to her."

"Wait!" Nancy said.

But Molly didn't wait. She marched across the street and ran up to Melissa.

"Hi!" Melissa said. She smiled, and her dimples showed. "Do you guys want to help shovel?"

"No, we do *not* want to help shovel," Molly snapped. "We're here to find out exactly where you got those earmuffs!"

"At the park," Melissa said. She gave Nancy a puzzled look. She didn't seem to understand why Molly was being so rude.

"That's exactly where I lost mine!" Molly announced.

"Oh," Melissa said. "Then I bet those are yours. Hold on a second. Let me get them for you."

Melissa went over to the snowman. She jumped up and got the earmuffs. Then she handed them to Molly.

55

Molly put her hands on her hips. "Did you find anything else at the park?" she asked.

Melissa shook her head.

"That's impossible," Molly said. "Because I left these earmuffs under my sled. My *stolen* sled."

"Well, I found them lying in the snow," Melissa said. "Although there *was* a sled nearby. An old pink saucer. Is that the sled you're looking for?"

"No," Molly said. "My sled was brand-new."

Melissa shrugged. "The pink saucer was the only sled I saw," she said. "At first I thought the earmuffs might belong to whoever owned it. But I asked around and found out they didn't. That's why I brought them home and put them on my snowman."

"Who did you ask about the ear-muffs?" Nancy asked.

Melissa thought for a second. "Um, Sam McCorry. He was waiting for some of his friends to come up the hill. He told me the pink saucer belonged to a girl he knew. He said the earmuffs weren't hers."

Molly stopped looking angry and started looking confused. "I give up," she said. "It seems as if my sled just vanished."

"Come on," Nancy said. "Let's go talk to Sam. Maybe he saw whoever took your sled."

Molly frowned thoughtfully. "Or maybe he took it," she said.

Nancy shook her head. "I don't think so," she said. "Sam already has an identical one."

"Maybe he got mixed up," Melissa suggested. "He could have taken Molly's sled by accident."

"That should be easy to prove," Nancy said to Molly. "You'd just have to show Sam where you wrote your name on the sled."

Molly's face fell. "Actually, I didn't write my name on it. I forgot."

"Well, let's go over to the McCorrys'

anyway," Nancy suggested. "If Sam isn't around, we can talk to Laura." Laura was Sam's younger sister. She was in the third grade, too.

Molly and Nancy said goodbye to Melissa. Then they walked over to the McCorrys'. Sam and Laura lived right across the street from Rebecca.

As the girls were walking up the McCorrys' driveway, an old car pulled in. A girl got out. Nancy recognized her. She was the same girl who had been sledding with Sam.

"I bet that's Sam's girlfriend," Molly whispered.

"Why?" Nancy asked.

"Look at her jacket," Molly whispered.

The girl was wearing a jacket that said River Heights High School Football.

That's Sam's jacket, Nancy thought. She was surprised Sam had given it away. He wore it every day all winter.

Nancy and Molly walked up to the

McCorrys' porch. Sam's friend had just rung the bell.

"Hey," the older girl said.

"Hi," Nancy said back.

Laura opened the door. "Hi, Angela," she said.

"Hey, squirt," the girl replied. "Where's Sam?"

"In by the TV," Laura said. "Hi, you guys!" she added to Nancy and Molly. "What's up?"

"We're trying to find Molly's lost sled," Nancy said. "We thought you might be able to help."

"Sam might have seen whoever took it," Molly added.

"Come in," Laura said. "You can ask Sam yourselves."

"Are you sure it's okay?" Molly asked. She lowered her voice. "I mean, his girl-friend is here."

Laura laughed. "Angela isn't Sam's girlfriend," she said. "They're just friend friends."

"Then how come she's wearing Sam's jacket?" Nancy asked.

Laura smiled. "Angela won it," she said. "She beat Sam sledding at the Gulch. Sam is *so* mad. He loves that jacket."

Nancy thought back to the afternoon before. She had seen Sam race against Angela. His sled was really fast. So how had Angela won?

An image popped into Nancy's mind. She saw Angela sledding up to where Sam had knocked Bess over. She was riding . . . a pink saucer!

Nancy grabbed Molly's hand. "Come on," she said. "We have to talk to Angela. I think she's the one who took your sled!"

8

Snow Ice Cream

Laura led the way into the McCorrys' den. Angela and Sam were sitting on the couch. A plate of snacks was on the table in front of them. They were watching a cartoon on TV.

"Angela," Laura said. "My friends want to talk to you."

Molly looked at Nancy. "Go ahead," she whispered.

Nancy cleared her throat. "Molly's sled is missing," she told Angela. "Do you have any idea where it is?"

Angela sat up straighter. She looked a bit embarrassed.

Sam sat up, too. He lowered the sound on the TV. He gave Nancy a big smile.

"A sled just like Sam's?" Angela asked. "One that was left under the oak tree near the sidewalk at the park?"

"That's it!" Molly said.

"I never saw it," Angela said.

Molly's shoulders slumped.

Angela laughed. "I'm just kidding," she said.

Sam gave Angela a push. "Stop teasing," he said. "Go on and tell Laura's friends how you managed to beat me sledding."

"All right, all right," Angela said. "I did see your sled. In fact, I kind of borrowed it."

"It's not borrowing if you don't ask first," Molly said.

Angela's face turned slightly pink. "I guess that's true," she said. "But one of the kids at the park said you wouldn't mind."

"What kid?" Nancy asked.

"Um, Carl Minelli's little brother," Angela said. "I don't know his name."

"Mike!" Nancy and Molly said together.

"I knew he had something to do with this," Molly added.

"Well, he didn't have *much* to do with it," Angela said. "He just told me you were letting everyone borrow your sled. I thought you wouldn't mind if I took it up to the Gulch. We were only gone about half an hour."

"I wouldn't have minded *if* you had asked first," Molly said. "And I still don't understand why you didn't return it."

Angela shrugged. "I did. But when we got back to the park, you were gone. So was Mike. I didn't know where to find you. Your name isn't on the sled anywhere."

"That's true," Molly said. "But do you think I could get my sled back now?"

"Sure," Angela said. "It's still in the trunk of my car. I'll get it right away."

Nancy, Laura, and Molly followed Angela outside. Angela unlocked her trunk and lifted out the sled.

"Yippee!" Molly yelled. She gave Nancy a big hug. "Thank you so much. I never would have found it without you."

"You're welcome," Nancy said.

"I'm sorry you were worried about it," Angela said. "I guess I should have tried harder to find you."

"That's okay," Molly said. "I'm going to put my name on the sled as soon as I get home." She turned to Nancy. "But first it's time for your reward."

Nancy smiled. "Snow ice cream," she said. "We can make it at my house. There's lots of clean snow in the back-yard."

"Sounds yummy," Laura said. "Can I come, too?"

"Sure," Nancy said. "We need to go find Bess and George over on Main Street. And let's get Rebecca and Melissa, too. I'll ask Hannah and my dad if I can have everyone over for din-ner. Since it's Friday, I don't think they'll mind."

Molly laughed. "Sounds good to me," she said. "Now that I have my sled back, I'm ready for a party!"

All of Nancy's friends gathered at her house. Molly showed the other girls how to make snow ice cream.

Nancy and George went into the Drews' backyard to get the snow. They scooped up some that wasn't right on top or too close to the ground.

Molly carefully folded the snow into the other ingredients. Then they put the snow ice cream into the freezer.

"Just in time for dinner!" Hannah said.

Dinner was yummy spaghetti and vegetables. The girls ate at the dining-room table with Nancy's father. Mr. Drew even let Nancy light some candles.

After everyone finished eating, the girls did the dishes together. By then the snow ice cream was ready to come out of the freezer.

Nancy put the bowl in the middle of the kitchen table. She gave each of her friends a spoon.

"You should have the first bite," Molly told Nancy. "After all, it is your reward."

"Okay," Nancy agreed. She took a spoonful and tried it. The snow ice cream wasn't as smooth as store-bought ice cream, but it was sweet and cold. And it tasted a little bit like the outdoors.

"Is it good?" Molly asked.

"Yummy for the tummy!" Nancy said. "Dig in!"

While the other girls started to eat, Nancy ran upstairs. She got her blue notebook and came back to the kitchen.

"What are you writing?" Rebecca asked between bites.

"Something that will help me remember this mystery," Nancy said. She began to write.

Molly's Snow Ice Cream

½ cup of heavy cream
1 tablespoon vanilla
½ cup powdered sugar
2 quarts of very clean snow

Put the cream into a mixing bowl.
Whip with a beater until fluffy. Add the
vanilla and sugar. Gently fold in the
snow. Cover and put into freezer until
ice cream hardens.

P.S. Snow ice cream tastes best after
solving a mystery.

Case closed, Nancy thought. "Hey,"
she added out loud. "Save some of that
for me!"

Do your younger brothers and sisters want to read books like yours?

Let them know there are books just for them!

THE NANCY DREW NOTEBOOKS ®

#1 The Slumber Party Secret

#2 The Lost Locket

#3 The Secret Santa

#4 Bad Day for Ballet

#5 The Soccer Shoe Clue

#6 The Ice Cream Scoop

#7 Trouble at Camp Treehouse

#8 The Best Detective

#9 The Thanksgiving Surprise

#10 Not Nice on Ice

#11 The Pen Pal Puzzle

#12 The Puppy Problem

#13 The Wedding Gift Goof

#14 The Funny Face Fight

#15 The Crazy Key Clue

#16 The Ski Slope Mystery

#17 Whose Pet Is Best?

#18 The Stolen Unicorn

#19 The Lemonade Raid

#20 Hannah's Secret

#21 Princess on Parade

#22 The Clue in the Glue

#23 Alien in the Classroom

#24 The Hidden Treasures

#25 Dare at the Fair

#26 The Lucky Horseshoes

#27 Trouble Takes the Cake

#28 Thrill on the Hill

Look for a brand-new story every other month

Available from Minstrel® Books
Published by Pocket Books

1356-02

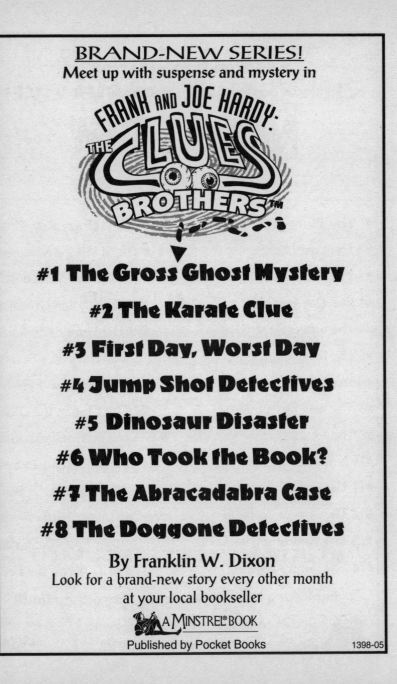

BRAND-NEW SERIES!

Meet up with suspense and mystery in

FRANK AND JOE HARDY: THE CLUES BROTHERS™

#1 The Gross Ghost Mystery

#2 The Karate Clue

#3 First Day, Worst Day

#4 Jump Shot Detectives

#5 Dinosaur Disaster

#6 Who Took the Book?

#7 The Abracadabra Case

#8 The Doggone Detectives

By Franklin W. Dixon

Look for a brand-new story every other month
at your local bookseller

A MINSTREL® BOOK

Published by Pocket Books   1398-05

TAKE A RIDE
WITH THE KIDS ON BUS FIVE!

Natalie Adams and James Penny have just started
third grade. They like their teacher, and they like
Maple Street School. The only trouble is, they have
to ride bad old Bus Five to get there!

#1 THE BAD NEWS BULLY
Can Natalie and James stop the bully on Bus Five?

#2 WILD MAN AT THE WHEEL
When Mr. Balter calls in sick,
the kids get some strange new drivers.

#3 FINDERS KEEPERS
The kids on Bus Five keep losing things.
Is there a thief on board?

#4 I SURVIVED ON BUS FIVE
Bad luck turns into big fun
when Bus Five breaks down in a rainstorm.

BY MARCIA LEONARD
ILLUSTRATED BY JULIE DURRELL

 A MINSTREL® BOOK
Published by Pocket Books

1237-04

FULL HOUSE™
Michelle

#5: THE GHOST IN MY CLOSET 53573-0/$3.99
#6: BALLET SURPRISE 53574-9/$3.99
#7: MAJOR LEAGUE TROUBLE 53575-7/$3.99
#8: MY FOURTH-GRADE MESS 53576-5/$3.99
#9: BUNK 3, TEDDY, AND ME 56834-5/$3.99
#10: MY BEST FRIEND IS A MOVIE STAR!
(Super Edition) 56835-3/$3.99
#11: THE BIG TURKEY ESCAPE 56836-1/$3.99
#12: THE SUBSTITUTE TEACHER 00364-X/$3.99
#13: CALLING ALL PLANETS 00365-8/$3.99
#14: I'VE GOT A SECRET 00366-6/$3.99
#15: HOW TO BE COOL 00833-1/$3.99
#16: THE NOT-SO-GREAT OUTDOORS 00835-8/$3.99
#17: MY HO-HO-HORRIBLE CHRISTMAS 00836-6/$3.99
MY AWESOME HOLIDAY FRIENDSHIP BOOK
(An Activity Book) 00840-4/$3.99
FULL HOUSE MICHELLE OMNIBUS 02181-8/$6.99
#18: MY ALMOST PERFECT PLAN 00837-4/$3.99
#19: APRIL FOOLS 01729-2/$3.99
#20: MY LIFE IS A THREE-RING CIRCUS 01730-6/$3.99
#21: WELCOME TO MY ZOO 01731-4/$3.99
#22: THE PROBLEM WITH PEN PALS 01732-2/$3.99
#23: MERRY CHRISTMAS, WORLD! 02098-6/$3.99

A MINSTREL® BOOK
Published by Pocket Books

Simon & Schuster Mail Order Dept. BWB
200 Old Tappan Rd., Old Tappan, N.J. 07675

Please send me the books I have checked above. I am enclosing $_____(please add $0.75 to cover the
postage and handling for each order. Please add appropriate sales tax). Send check or money order--no cash or C.O.D.'s please. Allow up to
six weeks for delivery. For purchase over $10.00 you may use VISA: card number, expiration date and customer signature must be included.
Name _____
Address _____
City _____ State/Zip _____
VISA Card # _____ Exp.Date _____
Signature _____

1033-28

Sabrina
The Teenage Witch™

Salem's Tails™

What's it like to be a powerful warlock,
sentenced to one hundred years in a
cat's body for trying to take over the world?

Ask Salem.

**Read all about Salem's magical
adventures in this new series based on
the hit ABC-TV show!**

#1 CAT TV
#2 Teacher's Pet
Salem Goes to Rome
#3 You're History

Now available!
Look for a new title every other month

A MINSTREL® BOOK
Published by Pocket Books

2007-02